SECRET
AGENT MAN

S.A.M. is digging for the
Lost City of Raisins. . . .

He is tracking down the treacherous green spitting bug,

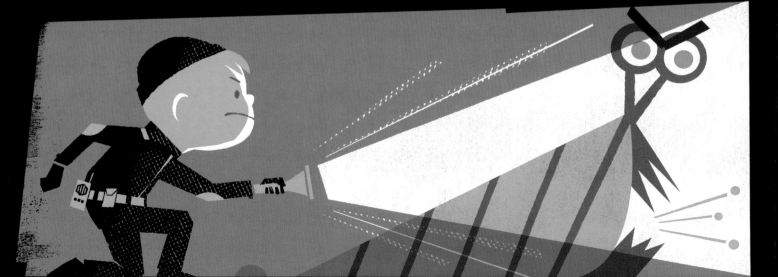

balancing on high places,

and stealing home.

K. is hanging out clouds.
"You need new shoes," says K.

To my three wonderful children,
who all learned to tie their shoes,
eventually
T. W.-J.

To Mom and Dad
B. W.

Text copyright © 2016 by Tim Wynne-Jones
Illustrations copyright © 2016 by Brian Won

First edition 2016

Library of Congress Catalog Card Number 2015934757
ISBN 978-0-7636-7119-8

 MIX
Paper from
responsible sources
FSC® C020056

LEO 21 20 19 18 17 16
10 9 8 7 6 5 4 3 2 1

Printed in Heshan, Guangdong, China

This book was typeset in Caecilia Bold.
The illustrations were created digitally.

Candlewick Press
99 Dover Street
Somerville, Massachusetts 02144

visit us at www.candlewick.com

SECRET AGENT MAN

GOES SHOPPING FOR SHOES

TIM WYNNE-JONES

illustrated by BRIAN WON

CANDLEWICK PRESS

S.A.M. and K. go shopping for shoes.

"I can't decide whether I want rocket shoes or vanishing shoes," says S.A.M.

"I'll be right with you, ma'am," says Shoe Store Man.

"That's K.," says S.A.M. "Short for Kay."

Shoe Store Man looks shifty.
"Frisk him," says S.A.M.

S.A.M. tries on lots of shoes.

"I'll take the ones with tiger stripes," says S.A.M.

"I'll have the same," says K.

S.A.M. watches Shoe Store Man tie his laces.
One bow, two bows. Over, under, and pull them tight.

"How about lunch?" says K.

He orders the double buffalo burger with
a side of snakes and an electron float.

"We are matching tigers," he says.

On the bus home, someone tries to steal
the Plans for World Domination.

"Oh, no, you don't," says S.A.M.

"Phew! That was close," says K.

"I feel woozy," says S.A.M. "Someone must have slipped something bad into my float."

"I'd suggest forty winks," says K.

"Make that twenty-seven winks," says S.A.M.
"I've got an important meeting."

He watches K. untie his shoelaces. One bow.
Then the other.

S.A.M. dreams of beautiful poisonous butterflies
and dangerous inflatable frogs.

His important meeting goes well.

"These are the Plans for World Domination," he tells his Team of Expert Spies. "Decode them and have the results on my desk by three."

"Will do," says Agent Coyote.

"Yes, sir," says Agent Ted.

"Three on the nose," says Agent Pig.

"Good," says S.A.M., and goes looking for K.

Chamber of
Silence.

She's not in
the Holding Cell
of Despair.

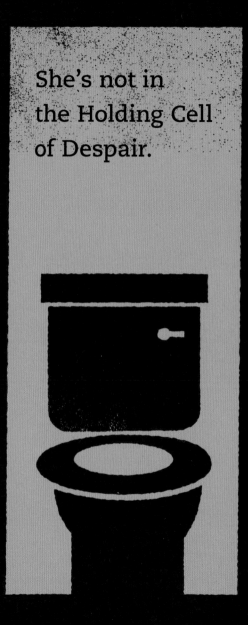

She's not in
the Torture
Chamber . . .

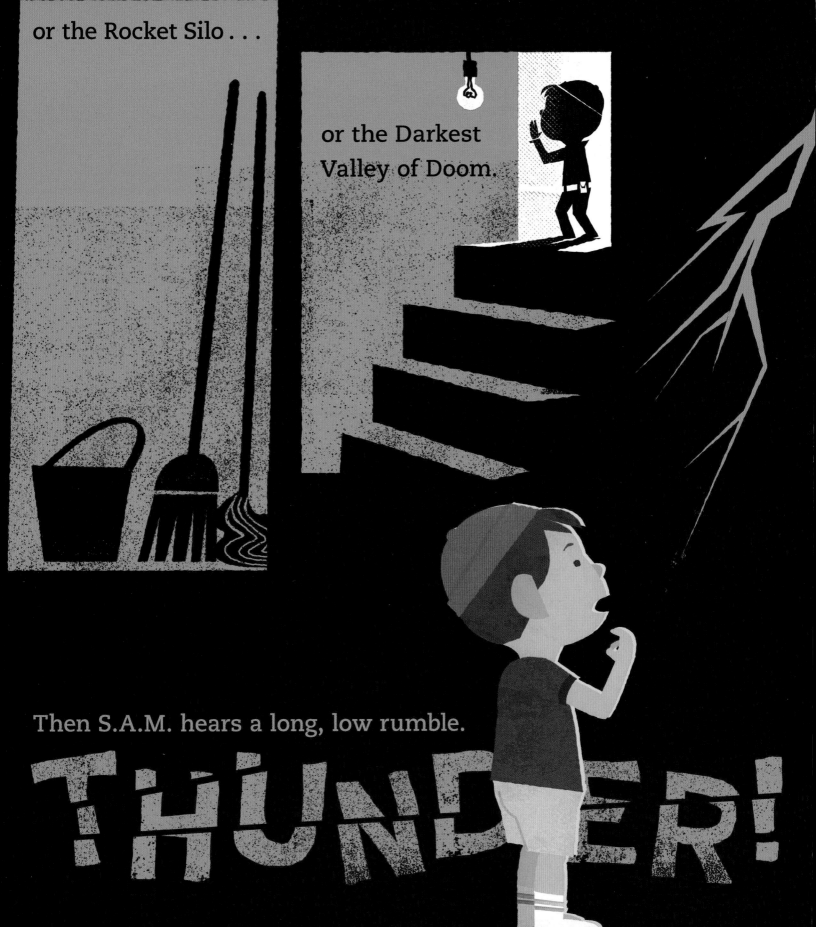

or the Rocket Silo . . .

or the Darkest Valley of Doom.

Then S.A.M. hears a long, low rumble.

THUNDER!

"Uh-oh," he says. Quickly he puts on
his new shoes and runs as fast as
a tiger to the rescue.

K. is bringing in the clouds.

"Let me help!" shouts S.A.M.

"Phew! That was close," says K.

They sit and watch the storm, drinking steaming mugs of lava topped with dollops of candied gardenia and pearls.

"Lucky my Team of Expert Spies warned me about the storm," says S.A.M.

"T.O.E.S," says K.

"Right," says S.A.M. "We're ready for anything."

"Good," says K.

S.A.M. looks at his new tiger shoes. They look very excited and proud.

"S.A.M.," says K, "did you tie your own shoelaces?"

"ROAR!"

says S.A.M.